PLAYDATE PALS

Alligator is
ANGRY

Rosie Greening • Dawn Machell

make
believe
ideas

It was a dark, rainy day and Bear and **Alligator** were deciding what to play.

"I know, let's paint some colorful flowers to brighten up this room!" said Bear.

"Good idea!" said **Alligator**.

The friends ran
to get their aprons.

Alligator wanted the red apron,
but Bear took it first.

"That's mine!" thought **Alligator**.
He **clenched** his teeth,
starting to feel **angry**.

Next the animals went to the art table.
Bear sat so close to **Alligator** that their
pictures touched.

"Move over!" snapped **Alligator**,
and he **pushed** Bear away.

Soon **Alligator** was painting
a big, yellow flower.
He was just finishing the last petal
when Bear took the yellow paint.

"I need that!" thought **Alligator**,
and his face started to get **hot**.

Alligator looked at his painting.
He didn't like it, and the more he looked
at it, the **hotter** and **angrier** he felt.

"I **want** the yellow paint!"
exploded **Alligator**.

He **grabbed** the paint
and it spilled on both paintings!

"My painting is ruined!" yelled **Alligator**. He felt a rush of **hot anger** burst out of his body.

He reached forward angrily
and **pinched** Bear!

Alligator ran away from the table. His heart was **beating fast**, and he was **breathing hard**.

But when he looked back,
he saw that Bear was **crying**.

Alligator took a **deep breath** and started to **calm** down. He didn't like seeing Bear cry. It made him **feel bad**.

Alligator went back to the table
and said, "I'm **sorry**, Bear.
I didn't mean to make you **sad**."

"That's ok – I get **angry** sometimes, too,"
said Bear, and they started painting
a picture together.

They **shared** the table and took turns using the yellow paint.

When Bear and **Alligator** had finished their painting, they put it on the wall.

It was beautiful, and it filled the room with color!

READING TOGETHER

Playdate Pals have been written for parents, caregivers, and teachers to share with young children who are beginning to explore the feelings they have about themselves and the world around them.

Each story is intended as a springboard to emotional discovery and can be used to gently promote further discussion around the feeling or behavioral topic featured in the book.

Alligator is Angry is designed to help children recognize their own feelings of anger and how they behave when they are angry. Once you have read the story together, go back and talk about any experiences the children might share with Alligator. Practice talking about your feelings together and encourage children to do so in other trusted relationships.

Look at the pictures

Talk about the characters. Are they smiling, frowning, or shouting? Help children think about what people look like or how they move their bodies when they are angry.

Words in bold

Throughout each story there are words highlighted in bold type. These words specify either the **character's name** or useful words and phrases relating to feeling **angry.** You may wish to put emphasis on these words or use them as reminders for parts of the story you can return to and discuss.

Questions you can ask

To prompt further exploration of this feeling, you could try asking children some of the following questions:

- When you are angry, what does it feel like in your body?
- What makes you feel angry and how do you show it?
- How do you feel when your friends are angry?
- Can you make an angry face?